FIRE ENGINES TO THE RESCUE

By Janet Campbell
Illustrated by Courtney Studios
With appreciation to the Joplin Fire Department

A GOLDEN BOOK • NEW YORK
Western Publishing Company, Inc., Racine, Wisconsin 53404

It is morning in the city—time for roll call at
Fire Company Number 2.
   Ten fire fighters line up outside the firehouse.
The lieutenant calls out their names.
   "Here!" says each fire fighter.
   The fire fighters from the night shift are going
home to get a good day's sleep.
   "Good luck," they call to the day fire fighters.

After roll call, the fire fighters check their gear. They each have a coat that protects them from both water and heat. It is called a turnout coat. They have rubber boots to keep their feet dry. They each have a hard helmet to protect their head from falling objects.

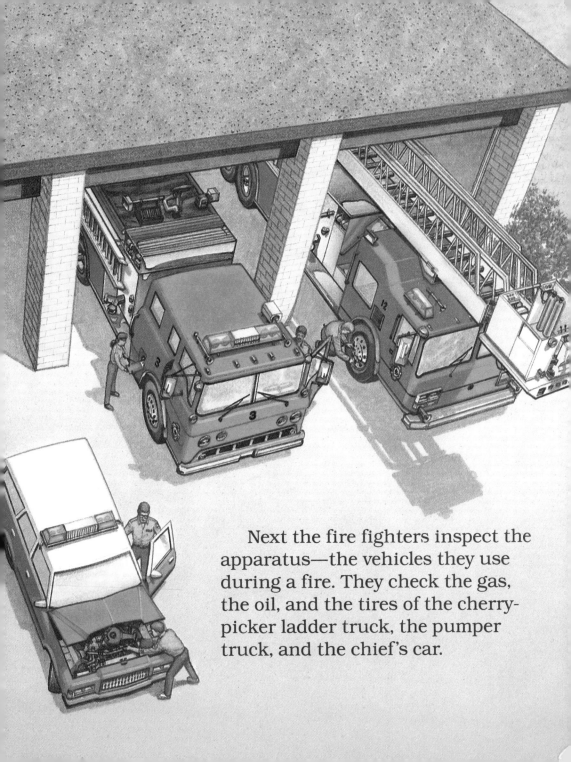

Next the fire fighters inspect the apparatus—the vehicles they use during a fire. They check the gas, the oil, and the tires of the cherry-picker ladder truck, the pumper truck, and the chief's car.

The fire fighters check the controls that work the cherry-picker bucket. They also check the ladders.

There is lots of equipment on the ladder truck. One fire fighter checks the axes. Another checks the hooks attached to long poles. A third fire fighter checks the power saw stored on the truck.

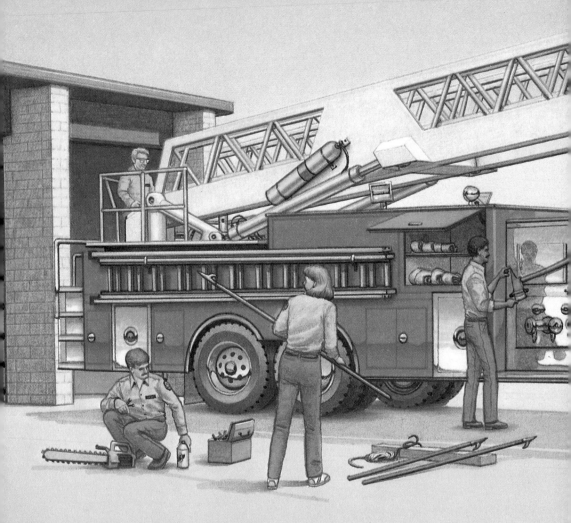

The breathing masks are inspected to make sure the tanks are full of air.
Is Ladder Truck Number 12 ready? Yes!

The pumper truck carries everything the fire fighters need for spraying water on a fire.

The crew checks the hoses to make sure they are not tangled. They test the pump and the pressure gauges. Then they check the breathing masks.

Is Pumper Truck Number 3 ready? Yes!

But there are other kinds of work to do, too.

Upstairs in the firehouse kitchen, one fire fighter takes his turn making lunch. He is cooking soup.

Downstairs, two fire fighters fix some of the small equipment. One puts a new handle on an ax. The other replaces the pole that holds a hook.

Three fire fighters practice first aid.

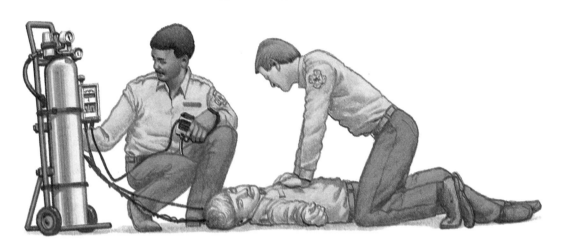

One fire fighter is on house watch, waiting for a fire signal. Suddenly a buzzer sounds. A computer printout is coming in from central dispatch.

"Fire Company Number 2—fire in progress—Sawyer's apartment complex—Broadway and 12th Streets."

The fire bell rings. Some of the fire fighters come sliding down the shiny brass pole.

All the fire fighters put on their coats and helmets. They step out of their shoes, pull on their big rubber boots, and jump onto the apparatus.

Sirens wail, lights flash, bells clang. The chief's car speeds out of the firehouse. Pumper Truck Number 3 and Ladder Truck Number 12 are right behind it.

At the fire, the chief tells his fire fighters what to do. One fire fighter connects the pumper truck to the hydrant. Then she opens the hydrant with a wrench.

Two other fire fighters unroll the hoses. Another turns on the pump when the hoses are in place.

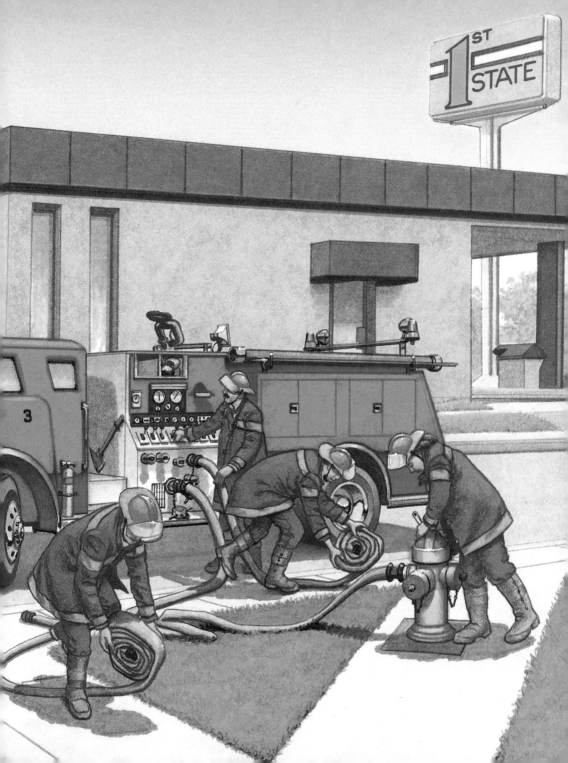

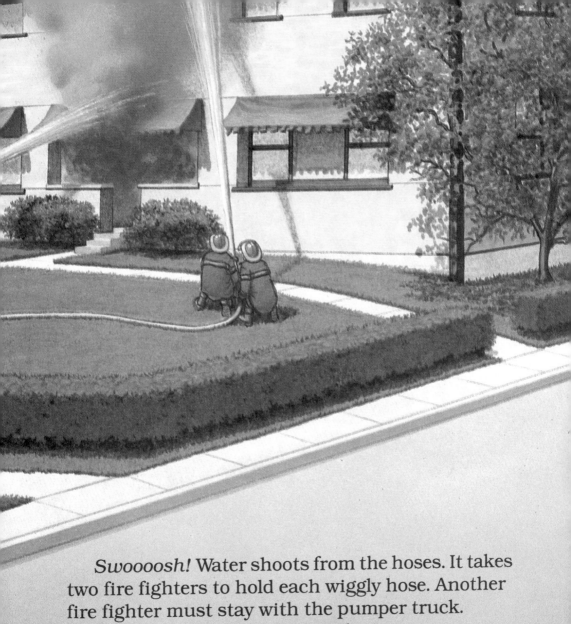

Swooooosh! Water shoots from the hoses. It takes two fire fighters to hold each wiggly hose. Another fire fighter must stay with the pumper truck.

Sssssss! The fire hisses with steam.

The crew from Pumper Truck Number 3 is hard at work, trying to put out the fire.

The crew of Ladder Truck Number 12 is busy, too.
One fire fighter pulls down a burning awning
with a hook, so it won't fall on anyone.
One fire fighter breaks windows with an ax before
the heat makes the glass explode.
Another fire fighter cuts a hole in the roof with
a power saw to let out smoke.

Look! Two people are trapped on the fire
escape. Flames are shooting up from below!
"Get that bucket up there!" shouts the chief.
One fire fighter climbs into the cherry-picker
bucket. Up it goes, all the way to the fourth floor.
Another fire fighter climbs down from the roof
to help the people into the bucket.

The bucket takes the people safely down to the ground.

Hurray for the brave fire fighters!

The fire fighters give the people oxygen to help them breathe. Then an ambulance comes to take them to the hospital.

The people are going to be all right.

The fire has been put out. Pumper Truck Number 3 and Ladder Truck Number 12 have returned to the firehouse.

First the tired fire fighters clean the apparatus. Then they put their gear away.

Next the fire fighters go to their lockers and put on clean, dry clothes.

It is way past lunchtime, but the cook still has to feed the hungry fire fighters.

"Soup's on!" he shouts to the ones who still haven't come upstairs.

And the fire fighters eat up every last spoonful.